OTTERS VS BADGERS

For Emilie
and Ben

OXFORD
UNIVERSITY PRESS

Great Clarendon Street, Oxford OX2 6DP

Oxford University Press is a department of the University of Oxford.
It furthers the University's objective of excellence in research,
scholarship,and education by publishing worldwide. Oxford is a
registered trade mark of Oxford University Press in the UK and in
certain other countries

Database right Oxford University Press (maker)

First published 2022

British Library Cataloguing in Publication Data available

ISBN: 978-0-19-277780-5

1 3 5 7 9 10 8 6 4 2

Printed in China

Paper used in the production of this book is a natural, recyclable
product made from wood grown in sustainable forests.
The manufacturing process conforms to the environmental
regulations of the country of origin

ANYA GLAZER

OTTERS VS BADGERS

OXFORD
UNIVERSITY PRESS

Before our story begins, there are a
few things you should know.

Firstly, the otters live on one side of the river.

Secondly, the badgers live on the other side of the river.

Thirdly, and MOST importantly . . .

Head otter

OTTERS
AND
BADGERS

DO NOT GET ALONG.

Head badger →

It's just the way things had always been.

Badgers and otters couldn't even share the river without a fight.

And it was only getting worse.

So, to avoid any more trouble, the leaders decided the two groups must never meet.

No badgers and no otters must EVER cross the river.

But our story really begins with an otter named Francie. The important things you need to know about Francie are:

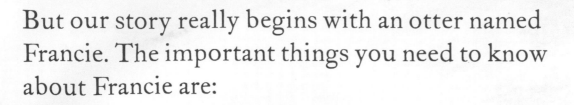 Firstly, she lives on the otter side of the river. (But you probably guessed that.)

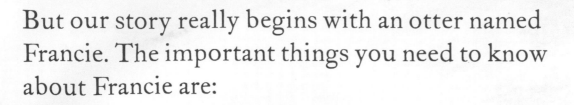 Secondly, she's a little shy.

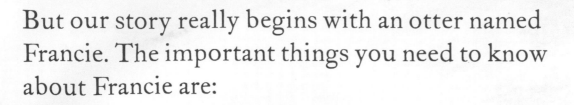 Thirdly, and especially: she bakes the best cakes anywhere along the river.

All the otters said so.

Francie was happiest
dreaming up recipes,

finding new flavours,

tasting and testing,

always in pursuit of the
perfect bake.

And one day,

when she was searching for

just the right ingredient for her
next creation,

HOP
HOP

she went a little farther...

. . . than she meant to.

Before the badgers could catch her,
Francie ran back to the otter side of
the river and the safety of her kitchen.

But the badgers were just a few steps behind.

When the badgers turned up on the otter side,
they demanded to see the otter with the muffins
who had been stealing their berries.

She was sneaking
onto OUR land!
She must pay!

Meanwhile, back in her kitchen,
Francie measured and mixed,

and stretched and shaped.

Because no matter what
trouble might be brewing . . .

. . . Francie always baked.

Francie's cookies were her best yet.

But although she never meant for her baking to
start another argument . . .

Suddenly, all eyes were on Francie.

Why can't we just share it all?

And everyone listened to what she had to say.

So now, this is where the otters AND the badgers live.
Together. On both sides of the river.

They still argue sometimes (everyone does).

But there is one thing they ALWAYS agree on . . .

Francie bakes the best cookies (and cakes,
and pies and muffins, too) along the whole river.